THE LOVE OF A THUG, THE PRICE OF A QUEEN

J-TWO

T&J
Publications

The Love of A Thug, The Price of A Queen
Copyright © 2020 by J-TWO

For more information, email tjpublicationspresents@gmail.com.

CHAPTER 1

AFTER FIVE LONG YEARS, I was finally being released from the Michigan Department Of Corrections. Shit seemed so unreal as I walked down the cell block for the last time. I was never coming back to this shit again is what I told myself as the guard led me up to the control center to be released. I took one last look back at the niggas on the yard. Everything inside these walls would remain the same day to day, and now I was going from this jungle of bars to the craziness of the free world.

"Good luck, Mr. Thomas." The guard said as he unlocked the gate to my freedom awaited me.

"I appreciate it." I paused and took a deep breath before walking out the gate. The air seemed fresher, and I thought the birds were singing extra loud as I took each step of freedom. The sky was cloudless and the sun was shining bright. I felt like I was being reborn as I took my first few steps of freedom.

After taking in the moment, I saw an all white Beamer 745 parked out in the parking lot. When Snow hopped out to welcome me home, I knew I would be straight. He was dipped in ice from head to toe, wearing designer all the way to his socks. Snow was my running mate from before I got knocked on the armed robbery I went down for.

When I left, he was a jack boy just like me but in the years of my absence, he had risen up in the streets and was now one of the main coke distributors in the whole city. And he made it known with all the ice on him. Snow was also the only person other than my mom who made sure my books were straight at all times.

"Melly! What's good my nigga!" He stepped to me, pulling me in for a hug. Snow was a little dude compared to my six foot one inches. "You remember my brother, Lil' Tim, right?"

I remembered Lil' Tim, but he was more like Big Tim now. He was taller than I was and had muscles as if he had just got done doing a bid.

"Yeah, I remember him. What's good Tim?" I walked up to him and shook up with him. Little Tim had a scar on the side of his face that made him look tougher than ever. He rocked a low cut with a taper and had two chunky diamond earrings in his ears. Being related to Snow must have been paying off for him.

Tim tilted his head to the side as he shook my hand. "Welcome home, Melly. You're all Snow has been talking about for the last two months." He said that with a little hate in his voice. When I left the streets, Tim was fifteen so I didn't see at reason for him to dislike me, but after doing time, I could read a nigga with only a glance.

"Yo', throw that shit away, nigga. You know I'm going to get you right my nigga. I don't know why you brought that shit with you." Snow snatched the garbage bag I was carrying with a couple jogging fits in it and tossed it into the metal trash can on the walkway next to the cars.

"I gotta go see my shorty and my mom asap. It's been two years since I saw either one of my ladies, bro." I looked at Snow as he climbed into the driver's seat. Tim went to sit in the passenger seat, but Snow told him to get in the back. He shot me a quick mug as I got into the front seat before Snow pulled off.

Snow grabbed a blunt out his ashtray and fired it up. I didn't even hit the weed and was coughing like I had been smoking cigarettes for thirty years.

"Damn nigga, that shit loud as hell." I started fanning my hand in the air to clear the smoke from around me before cracking the window open to let the remainder out.

Snow looked in the rearview mirror smiling at his little brother. "You trying to hit this shit?" Snow asked, pushing the blunt towards me.

"Naw fam, I'm good right now." I wasn't about to pick up any habits until I could afford them. I knew better then to become addicted to anything without having the means to support the addiction. I was trying to stay sober until I got a good amount of cash.

"I'll hit it for his ass." Tim grabbed the blunt from him and took a big hit that sent him into a coughing fit. I guess his lungs weren't ready for the potent shit Snow was smoking. Looking into the backseat, I laughed at Tim whose eyes were watering from the pull on the blunt.

As we drove farther from the prison, I was slowly coming back into the reality that I would now have to find a way to provide for me and mine. Snow took me shopping at River Town Crossing, the biggest mall in the city. He made sure he let it be known that he was cashing out a nice amount of money on his homeboy who just made it out of the joint.

Every female that came by looked at him as if he was some sort of star, and being that I was walking with him, they were giving me a double take, too. I was feeling all the attention we were receiving as we shopped around the mall. Snow bought a few pairs of shoes and I had him grab me a hand full of Nike jogging outfits.

I made sure he hit my hand with a couple hundred dollars while we went around and the mall. I stopped and bought my daughter a stuffed animal from Build-A-Bear Workshop that said

Daddy Loves You when the paw was squeezed. I also got my mom some scented candles from Bath and Body Works. I couldn't come home empty handed to the two ladies in my life after being away so long. After Snow dropped the few dollars on me, I had him take me straight to my OG crib. I had to see the two most important people in my life.

༄

My mom had been living in the same house since I could remember; on the South Side of Grand Rapids. It wasn't a big house but she always told me it was hers and that's what mattered. The grass out front was a brownish green and looked like it hadn't been cut in months. The house had the appearance like no one even lived there. For some reason, I was nervous as I walked up the four short steps to the front door.

I twisted the handle opening the door as it hung loosely on its hinges. Stepping inside, instantly, I was taken back by the ill smell inside the house. It smelled like spoiled milk had been spilled everywhere. From the cobwebs in the corner of the entryway, I doubted the house had been dusted in forever. When I shut the door, I heard little footsteps running down the creaking stairs then I saw my baby girl, Arrieal. She had grown so much since the last time I saw her. I could hardly believe it was her.

"Daddy!" She screamed in a high pitch voice. She came down the stairs faster than I ever did as a child. The site of her brought tears to my eyes as emotions ran through me. I was more than happy to be home with my little angel.

"Baby girl! Look how big you've got, come here!" I was as excited to see her but her reaction to me walking through the door was more than I expected.

Her hair was undone and her clothes were too little for her long skinny limbs. It hurt me to see her like that. She was my princess and deserved everything in the world and then some. It was my fault that she was looking the way she was. I was her

Dad, the person who was supposed to support and protect her. She jumped up into my arms, wrapping herself around me as if she would never let me go.

As me and my baby continued our embrace, my mother walked from the kitchen with her hands over her mouth and tears in her eyes.

"Jermel, come give me a hug boy!" She squealed as she struggled on her feet to get over to us. I could tell that she wasn't in the best shape. Life had taken its toll on her. She had aged fast in the time I'd been gone. My mom had overcome a crack addiction that lasted ten years back when I was my daughter's age, until I was around sixteen years old. And after a handful of abusive relationships, she finally was able to find God and clean her life up. But with me as a child, I was surprised she made it to the age of 57.

"Momma; how are you doing, my love?" I squeezed her tiny frame into my arms and kissed her forehead. She smelled like fried food and Dial soap. She had on one of her signature wigs on that she wore to hide her age. Even through everything she had been through in her years, she was beautiful.

She put a big smile on her face as she leaned back so she could look me in my face "Oh, I'm doing fine. I'm even better now that you are home son. We need you out here."

My mom was never one to look for or want empathy from anyone and I knew it. "Well, I'm not going back so you don't have to worry about that, mom." From the look of things, I could tell that they needed me. The house was dim and it was hot as fuck in the crib. "Why is it so hot in here?" I had only been in the house for five minutes and sweat was starting to build up under my armpits.

Releasing me from her hug, she took a step away from me. "I couldn't pay the bills last week, baby. I'll have the money Friday to get it all worked out." She looked to the ground as if she was embarrassed. I knew she was working part time at a restaurant on 28th street. But it obviously wasn't paying her enough to pay the bills, take care of Arrieal and all the other things she needed around the house and for herself. I was sure, by looking over the situation, if it wasn't for food stamps they wouldn't have been eating.

I pulled her in for another hug as Arrieal held on to my leg. I wasn't going to let them continue to live like this. I was home now so I was going to make sure they had any and everything they wanted. "Don't worry, momma. I'm going to take care of it. I got you." I wasn't planning on jumping back in the streets right away, but looking at my mom and my daughter's situation I had no choice but to get it right away. When Snow came to get me tonight I was going to talk to him about getting some money ASAP.

"You hungry, baby? I can cook you something?" My mom asked, walking back towards the kitchen.

Looking down at my baby girl in the cheap, size-too-small clothes, I knew what I had to do. "Naw, I'm good, momma. I just want to spend time with you two." I picked up Arrieal and kissed her cheeks repeatedly causing her to laugh. In my head, I was angry with myself for leaving my mom to care for my baby with no help. After Arrieal's mom left her with me when she was only nine months old, I took care of her up until I went to prison when she was two. I was responsible for the way they were now living. And I was going to get them out of the poverty they were in.

I spent the day with my baby and mom until the sun went down and Arrieal fell to sleep.

❧

I had to get some money fast. I was waiting on the front steps looking at the star filled sky. It was a full moon out and my mind was racing trying to figure out how I was going to get my bands up right away. As I was waiting for Snow, in deep thought, my mom stepped out the house with a worried look on her face.

She took a deep breath and stood beside me on the steps. A light rain began to fall on us and the wind was starting to pick up.

"Jermel, don't you go out here getting into no trouble. Arrieal needs you out here. I need you out here, son. It has not been easy raising her by myself. I'm getting old, Jermel."

She had tears building in her eyes. I wanted to tell her I wasn't planning on getting involved in the streets but I couldn't sit down and let my two hearts live the way they were. I never lied to my mom and I wasn't going to start now.

"Mom, I gotta do what I gotta do to make sure y'all are good. I can't allow y'all to live like this. I'm home now, and it's my responsibility to make sure y'all are happy." Snow pulled into the driveway in his Beamer as me and my mom stood on the steps, getting wet as the rain began to come down heavier.

My mom looked like she was ready to ball up and cry. But she knew if I didn't provide for them then the way that they were living wouldn't change. She also knew what I was known to do in the streets. My name had rung bells throughout Grand Rapids since I was a young teen.

"Please son, don't leave us again. We need you with us. I'll be praying for you baby." I could see the tears forming in her eyes.

"I know y'all need me, mom. That's why I gotta do what I gotta do. I'll be back." I wasn't sure what I was going to get into, but I knew I was about to jump in the streets. I saw no other way to get a lot of money in a short period of time. I needed to get the electric back on and get my baby some new clothes. There was no way I was going to be fresh and my baby was running around all dirty. Under no circumstances was I going to let that happen.

She turned around and walked back in the house. Seeing her this way only fueled me to get some money into the household asap. Money couldn't buy happiness but it sure did make things seem better. As I stepped off the last step, I looked back at the house where I was raised to see my mom looking out the front window.

Rain beat down on the window as she watched me walk off. It was like a replay of the day I was arrested. She had begged me to stay out the streets that day and here I was again, ignoring her and jumping back into the streets that took me away before.

CHAPTER 2

"WHATS GOOD MY NIGGA?" Snow tried handing me the blunt he was smoking before putting it into the ashtray, but I waved it off. He must have seen enough of me and my moms exchange on the steps to notice something was wrong. "OG on yo ass already, huh?" Putting the car in gear, he began backing out the driveway.

"Shit fucked up, bro. I need to get some money like asap." Snow was already speeding up the block. The short talk with my Mom was replaying through my head. She was afraid to lose me again, but I wasn't going to let them continue to live like they were.

"Shit, that's all you gotta say. You know I got you my nigga. I can throw you a bag right now." Snow looked at me with a you know who I am type expression on his face. I know he could put me on but I ain't have time to sit in no trap. I needed money now. I was ready to get back on my jack boy shit.

I looked at Snow with all seriousness in my face as he drove towards his crib.

"I ain't got time to be serving bags, fool. I need a come up fast not slow. The way my baby and my OG living, ain't sitting right with me."

I saw no point in beating around the bush. The rain was

pouring down now and the sound of thunder could be heard over the Lil' Baby song he was playing through his speakers.

He looked at me to see if I was playing, but the look on my face told him that I was dead serious.

"Look, you know I hate that jack boy shit, Melly. But I think I can do something for you one time. You always been a straight goon, my nigga." He smiled pulling the smoking blunt out the ashtray and taking three strong pulls before exhaling the big yellowish cloud of smoke.

"You know I ain't ever been the type to sell dope. But I always had a way with them straps." I was one of the most ruthless niggas in our city coming up and those years in prison only turned me up to a whole 'nother level of savage. And the sight of how my daughter and mothers were living was bringing it out of me. I hadn't been out for a whole day and I was getting ready to jump into the deep end of the game.

❧

When we pulled up to Snow's house out in Kentwood, which was on the outskirts of Grand Rapids, the rain had stopped. Snow was living in a two story house that was all white. I would have never thought he would be living out here in the suburbs five years ago. He parked the Beamer next to an all white Range Rover that sat in the driveway. He was obviously living up to the name Snow with all his white whips.

I stepped out the car just as a Mint Green Charger pulled into the driveway. I turned around to see Lil' Tim jump out the Charger that was sitting on offset 26 inch chrome rims. The rain from earlier made the paint and chrome hit extra hard in the light from Snow's garage.

"What y'all old heads standing outside for?" Tim asked as he slammed his car door and walked towards us. His walk was more like a pimp stroll. Lil' Tim definitely thought he was a boss.

"Shut yo' punk ass up, nigga. You just hope you make it to see our age, nigga. Let's get in the crib, Melly, so we can talk this business." Snow walked towards the house.

I followed Snow into the house with Tim right behind. The all white theme continued on the inside of the house as well. Snow had an all white living room with small touches of red through it. But he walked past it and opened a door that went to the basement.

With each step I took down the stairs, the smell of kush increased. It smelled like a skunk had just sprayed the room with its foul scent. The basement was probably the only room that didn't go with the all white theme. It was a blackout. He had a large screen on the wall that was showing highlights of Zion Williamson dunking the ball.

Snow took a seat on the giant leather sectional couch and pulled out a cigar from the box on the table.

"Tim, go grab us a couple brews." Using a little tool, he clipped the end of the cigar as I took a seat on the couch.

Tim walked off with an attitude, but followed Snow's orders, running up the stairs to fetch beers for us all.

"So, I was thinking while we were on the way here; I know a spot you can hit. It should have some work in it and so cash." He lit up the cigar and took a few puffs to make sure the cherry on the end was fiery red. The smell of the cigar quickly took over the room, smelling of vanilla.

"I can care less about the dope, bro. Like I said, I need money."

Tim came down the stairs holding three bottles of beer in his hands. He handed me one then stepped over to Snow and set another on the table in front of him before sitting down and popping some sort of pill washing it down with his beer.

"Okay, how bout this. All the dope you get, I'll buy from you." He put the cigar into the big glass ashtray and picked the beer up, taking a sip. "But you gotta take Lil' Tim with you."

I almost spit the beer out my mouth. Snow knew how I

moved. I never needed no help. And being that I never been in any situations with Tim, I didn't like the idea.

Tim didn't even know what we were talking about, but I could tell by the look on his face he wasn't too interested in doing anything that involved me.

Setting the beer on the table, I searched for the right words to say without disrespecting Snow or Tim. "Bro, I know he yo' little brother, but you know I do shit solo. It's less of a risk." I leaned forward placing my elbows on my knees looking at Snow. He showed no emotion in his face. But before he could speak, Tim went in.

"Fuck you mean its less of a risk. I'm bout my business, nigga." He looked like he wanted to fight me and still didn't know what we were going to get into.

"Chill the fuck out, Tim. Look Melly, this my little brother. He's been asking me to put him on something forever, but I didn't want to risk him like that. But if he is with you he can see how shit goes and I know he will be taken care of. So it's either he goes with you or I can't put you on the lick." He picked his cigar back out the ashtray and began to puff on it blowing out smoke rings.

I had no choice, but to take him cause I needed the money that was going to come from the lick.

"Alright, that's cool. But he gotta listen to what I say when we do this." I looked at Tim who was about to say something until Snow cut him off.

"Bet. This lick should put you in a nice position, too." He placed the cigar back into the ashtray before breaking down the lick to me and his brother. From the way he made it seem, it would be a walk in the park and I would be up about twenty to thirty thousand.

It was a little after one in the morning when me and Lil' Tim pulled onto the block of the house that Snow put us on. Tim double checked the address in his phone as I glanced around the block. The night was quiet besides the barking of a couple dogs around the neighborhood. I could smell the moisture in the air through the open window. But clutching onto the Chrome .45, I was going to leave the smell of lead floating on the block.

Tim pointed to the only house on the block with lights on after checking the address in his phone.

"That's the house right there." He put his phone into the center console and pulled out his Glock .40 with a thirty clip sticking out the bottom longer than a baby leg.

I cocked back the slide on my .45 putting a hollow point into the chamber.

"Let's go get this money, fool." I stepped out of the car onto the wet concrete and instantly went into kill mode. I had nothing on my mind but getting to the money inside the house by any means. As we crept up to the house, low sounds of music could be heard coming from the house. Whoever was inside was obviously still up.

"We are going through the back door, follow me." Ducking under the window line, I ran down the side of the house with Tim on my heels.

We could hear voices on the inside followed by a loud obnoxious laugh. The back of the house was empty and luckily for us the back light wasn't on. I stepped to the door ready to boot it in when Tim stopped me.

"Let me kick the door in." He put his hand out as if he was moving me out the way before getting lined up to kick the door.

I brushed off him telling me what to do and got my gun ready to run inside. Tim took two big steps back to be able to put some power in his kick. Before he could lift his foot, I stepped in front of him, raised my foot and booted the door in.

Crash! The door flew in and I was in the house seconds after it hit the floor. The smell of weed was strong on the inside and the music was way louder than I thought. I expected someone to be rushing towards the sound of the door being kicked in. I paused holding my gun towards the hallway leading to the front of the house, but no one came.

As we crept up the hallway, a nigga crossed the hallway from a room and went into another door slamming it closed. I ran forward putting my ear to the door and heard the sound of the nigga pissing in the toilet. Tim cracked the door to the room he had come out of and started bucking his Glock. *Boom! Boom! Boom!* He entered the room just as the bathroom door I was standing in front of swung open.

"Say yo' prayers, my nigga." He ran into the barrel of my .45.

Ka-Boom! The big pistol barked, jerking my arm back. I blew his thoughts back into the bathroom. Brain matter splattered all over the sink and mirror as his lifeless body dropped to the floor. That was two dead now. Snow had warned us that there was usually two or three niggas in the house at all times.

Leaning into the room where Tim went into, I saw him rummaging through the closet.

"Go check upstairs!" I turned out the room and ran towards the room where music was blasting. Right when I was about to step into the main room of the house, gunfire erupted almost knocking my head off my shoulders. I fell to the floor as the bullets crashed into the wall sending wood splinters flying everywhere.

The shooter had some type of automatic cause he had let off what seemed like a hundred shots before I heard his magazine drop to the floor. I got off the floor and stepped in the room, shooting off my hip, catching him twice in his chest as he was sticking a fully loaded clip into his assault rifle.

I squeezed the trigger while I aimed at his midsection. *Ka-Boom! Ka-Boom!* The gun almost flew out my hands from all its power. He was slumped on the couch as blood oozed out the fist size holes in his chest. Sitting on the table were two bricks of raw cocaine, which looked like he was preparing to break down into smaller amounts. There was a triple beam scale and a box of sandwich bags next to the bricks. I grabbed the Nike backpack off the floor and stuffed the dope into it. All that was left to do was find the mony, and we could get the fuck on.

As I tossed the downstairs looking for the money that was supposed to be in the house, I heard a scream upstairs over the Future song that blasted through the speakers.

I swung the backpack over my shoulder and ran up the stairs skipping steps as I went up them. I could hear the sound of somebody tussling in the room at the top of the stairs. I kicked the door in and went in leading with my gun. Tim was on top of a light skin woman with his pants halfway down his ass.

He reached up and smacked the shit out of her.

"Bitch, stop fighting and I'll make it quick!" He gripped her by the neck and began to squeeze life out of her.

He grabbed a hold of her wife beater and snatched it off her with ease, exposing her bare breast. The nigga was trying to rape her in the middle of the robbery.

"Tim, get the fuck off her, nigga! What the fuck wrong with you!" I grabbed him by the back of his hoodie and pulled him off her. Her eyes were already swelling shut from the slapdown he delivered on her.

Getting to his feet, Tim lifted his gun pointing it at my face. "Nigga, we here to take what we want! And I want this little bitch right here." He was huffing and puffing like he just went ten rounds in a boxing ring. From the side of my eyes, I could see the woman reaching under the bed for something.

"So you gonna shoot me, lil' nigga?" I looked him in his empty eyes. He was going to kill me. He tightened his grip on the handle of his Glock.

I knew if I tried to lift my gun to shoot him first he would shoot me before I could even level my gun to him. All I could think about was my mom telling me not to leave the house. And now I was about to die in less than twenty four hours after being released.

Before I could even say anything, the woman sat up straight

on the bed with a big ass revolver in her hand aiming at the back of his head.

She closed her eyes. "Bitch ass nigga" She squeezed the trigger. *Boom!* Tim fell to the floor slowly as his brains painted my sweater. His face landed on my shoes and when I looked up the woman was pointing the gun at me, but she slowly dropped the gun onto the bed as tears flowed from her eyes.

CHAPTER 3

LOOKING DOWN at Tim's dead body as his blood poured out his head, I momentarily froze. *Karma is a mothafucka and he got what he deserved for trying to rape her,* I thought. Coming back from my quick withdrawal from reality, I looked over to the woman on the bed. For some reason, I found myself feeling for her. I knew I wasn't supposed to leave any witnesses but after almost being raped and then saving my life, I couldn't find it in me to kill her.

I walked up to her on the bed stepping over Tim's lifeless body. She started to reach for the gun again but I stopped her by grabbing her small hand. Her skin was soft and she had a pedicure with a stylish design on her nails. Looking up at me, I was drawn into her hazel eyes.

"You just saved my life, Ma and I'm thankful for that. That nigga got what he deserved for trying to do that to you. I ain't going to hurt you, but I need the money that's stashed here." I didn't know who she was or why she was in the trap but she had to know where the money was kept.

She placed her arm over her titties trying to cover herself the best she could as I stood over her. From the way she was shaking, I could tell she had never shot anyone before.

She shook her head from side to side,"I...I can't give it to you..He will kill me."

Whoever she was talking about obviously had her scared enough for her not to give up the money. I let go of her hand and snatched the big revolver she shot Tim with and tucked it in my waistband. I wasn't going to kill her, but I wasn't leaving without the money.

I began to trash the room looking for the money. I tossed each dresser drawer to the floor and stepped to the closet and began to go through every piece of her wardrobe.

Turning from the closet, I looked at her as my anger was building up. Thoughts of my baby flashed in my head. She must have thought I was getting ready to shoot her because she put her hands up as I stepped towards her.

"Okay! Okay! Please, just don't kill me!" The look on her face made me think of my mom back when she was younger. I would never hit a woman and her bruised eye was damn near closed from the smack Tim had laid on her. She got out the bed slowly then kneeled next to the bed reaching under the mattress.

"Don't even try nothing stupid, baby girl." I aimed my .45 at her back. After what she did to Tim, I had to be on point fucking with this chick.

She pulled a blueish metal box from under the bed and lifted it up setting it on the bed. I was still holding the gun on her when she looked at me and flinched.

"Please, don't shoot me. The money is in the box." Tears began to stream down her face again.

I lowered my gun and stepped closer to her. I could damn near feel the fear coming off her body. She started to twist the dial on the lock of the box. Once it clicked, she opened the box stepping to the side so I could see the rubber banded stacks inside.

I started to pull the money out the box, stuffing it into the backpack with the Bricks in it.

"You saved my life, Ma and I'll forever owe you for that." I looked back at her watching me put the money in the bag. She looked surprised by what I had said. The bass of a car system could be heard even over the music from down stairs and lights flashed by the window. The expression on her face changed immediately, fear taking over her.

She grabbed me by the arm and began to pull me towards the door of the room. "You gotta go! He is here; hurry up!"

I stuffed the last two stacks of cash into the backpack and followed her out the room down the stairs. I didn't understand why she was trying to help me get away after robbing her, but she was pulling me so hard I almost fell on top of her going down the stairs. When we got to the back door she stopped me from running out into the night gripping my shirt tightly.

"You said you owed me. So promise, when I send for you, you'll come." She stared into my eyes as if she could see my soul. I didn't know how she would find me, yet I nodded and tried to pull away from her grip.

She pulled me back closer to her, getting on her tiptoes to look me in my face. "Tell me you promise." A tear was forming in the one eye that wasn't swollen shut. It was like she was calling out to be saved.

Looking her in her eyes, I told her what I needed for me to get up outta there. "I promise you, I got you." I don't know why I didn't just snatch away and take off running. But something about the way she looked at me told me she needed my help.

"Okay, I'll get a hold of you. Now go!" She pushed me out the open door.

I disappeared into the night running faster than an Olympic sprinter. She didn't know my name or anything about me, but for some reason I felt like she would be getting in touch with me real soon. I ran down the alley as fast as I could trying to get away from the house. With two pistols, two kilos of coke and about thirty thousand dollars on me, I was a running Fed case.

I don't know what happens to your body but when you're running from something it's like you have everlasting stamina. I didn't stop running for thirty straight minutes, until I made it to Snow's block. Once I started walking, my lungs began to burn like I had a furnace in me. I didn't know what I would say or how to tell him his brother got killed during the lick, but I dreaded having to tell him. Because to me, he got what he deserved for trying to rape 'ol girl. I didn't condone killing women but if he had just bodied her things would have gone different.

The wind had started to pick up when I made it to Snow's driveway, walking past his Beamer and Range up to the front door. Ringing the doorbell, I waited for him to open the door. After a few minutes of waiting, I tried the handle and the door came open.

Stepping into the dark house, I called for him. "Snow! Where you at my nigga?" Walking down the hallway I could hear faint sounds coming from the basement.

I opened the door and stepped onto the stairs leading to the basement taking in the smell of one of Snow's vanilla cigars. When I made it to the landing, I saw Snow leaning to his side on the couch drooling as his cigar burned in his hand. On the table was a plate of tan powder with a rolled up dollar bill next to it. The nigga Snow had nodded off heroin.

I snatched the burning cigar out his hand as it was an inch from burning the couch. "Snow! Wake yo' ass up!" Stuffing the cigar out into the ashtray, I took a seat on the couch setting the backpack next to his plate of heroin.

His eyes opened into slits as his head bobbed like it was too heavy for him to hold up. "What's good, Melly?" His head was already sinking back down into his chest.

"I got two bricks from the lick. You still gonna buy this shit from me right?" I pulled out the two kilos leaving the money in the bag. The nigga was so high he began to snore. I clapped my hands next to his face waking him up again.

Scrunching up his face, he looked at me with a scowl. "Nigga, I heard you. Don't come in my crib blowing my high nigga shit. I'll buy the birds from you, fool. I'll give you thirty-five thousand for them." As soon as he stopped talking his head slowly began to fall to the side.

I wanted more than thirty-five for each kilo but with the money I got from the lick added to it, I would be able to get my mom and baby together all the way.

"Alright, bet. That will do." I slid the bricks closer to him on the table. I could have swore the nigga was sleeping but he got up from the couch and walked over to the TV stand all zombie like and reached behind it pulling out a shoebox. I was slightly tripping on the fact the nigga was snorting raw, but he was a grown ass man, and I was just trying to get some money to fix the problems at my OG crib.

He sat down on the couch with the box on his lap. His eyes didn't look open but he was mumbling words that made no sense to me. Even though he was high as hell, he had no trouble counting up the thirty-five thousand and tossing it to me.

I caught the stacks of money and put them into the backpack with the lick money. "Good looking, fam. I'm about to slide back to my mom's crib, fool. My baby is gonna want to see me when she wakes up."

The nigga had dozed back off and didn't reply. The keys to his Beamer were also on the table and I grabbed them after throwing the backpack over my shoulder. I left Snow's crib in his Beamer up about seventy thousand dollars. I didn't tell Snow his brother was dead, but he was so far gone snorting heroin, he never asked about his brother.

When I finally made it to my moms it was almost three in the morning. Stepping into the house, I walked to the couch and sat down tossing the backpack on the floor next to the coffee table that was covered in newspapers and *Life* magazines. I was sleeping in under five minutes after I sat on the couch. I went to sleep thinking about the shopping spree I was going to take my two ladies on.

❧

I woke up to my daughter jumping on top of me on the couch and my mom looking down on me from the other side of the coffee table.

"Daddy! Daddy! Wake up; me and Granny made you breakfast!" She had a smile so big on her face it caused me to smile. I wrapped my arms around her tiny body and put butterfly kisses all over her face.

"You cooked for me, baby? You're the best daughter in the whole wide world." I peppered her with a few more kisses before sitting up.

"Good morning, son. Come get you some food. Arrieal and I were in the kitchen all morning waiting for you to get up. She couldn't wait any longer." Smiling at me and my daughter hugging on the couch, she turned around and walked into the dining room.

I got up off the couch with Arrieal in my arms and followed her to the table full of food. They had made enough food for ten full grown men. There were at least twenty pancakes on a platter along with eggs and bacon to feed a football team.

"All this for me?" I eyed my mom setting Arrieal down.

She pulled out one of the old wooden chairs and sat down and started filling up her plate. "We thought you might be a little hungry." She sat down and began making a plate of her own.

I really was starving. "I am; thank you two beautiful ladies for the great meal." I took my seat and loaded my plate full of bacon and pancakes drenching them in syrup.

The food was so good I didn't talk for the next fifteen minutes as I stuffed my face. Washing down the food with a large cup of orange juice, I felt like my stomach was going to explode as I leaned back in the chair.

"Y'all ready to go shopping or what?" I looked from my mom to my daughter.

Arrieal was the first one to jump out her chair and say yes. My moms face told me that she wasn't happy with me leaving last night. She knew I had gone and did something I shouldn't have. But to me, I did what needed to be done. I had to make sure they were straight. I told my daughter to go get ready and helped my mom clean off the table. She didn't say anything and that spoke more volumes then any words she could have said.

After helping clean up, I went and showered before putting on one of the outfits Snow bought me. When I came downstairs, my mom and Arrieal were waiting by the door. Arrieal couldn't stop smiling, and even though my mom didn't approve of me jumping into the streets, she even looked happy to be getting out the dusty house.

I would make sure the house was taken care of after I got them both dipped in the latest fashion. I drove them in Snow's Beamer to River Town Crossing where Snow had taken me and cashed out and bought damn near the whole mall. I had to make three trips to the car to put the bags up. I dropped almost twenty thousand on clothes and shoes for my two ladies. And if they had wanted anything else, I would have spent the money on them without a doubt. I owed them both the world for leaving them without for those long five years.

After all the shopping, they must have been exhausted because before I got all the bags into the house they had fallen to sleep on the couch. I carried Arrieal up to her room and laid her on her bed and kissed her forehead. I had made my baby smile and that to me meant the world.

When I got back downstairs, my mom was sleeping on the couch. I walked to her room and set ten thousand on her dresser. She wasn't going to be working a job while I was free. I left her room and grabbed a broom out the hallway closet and began to clean the house up. After five years in prison, I had become a neat freak and I wouldn't be able to live in a house of filth. I was riding on cloud nine after seeing my two loves smile and get everything they wanted today. I would make sure they continued to smile as long as I had breath in my lungs.

CHAPTER 4

IT HAD BEEN two weeks since I did the robbery and things at my moms crib were a lot better. My daughter stayed smiling and my mom had that sparkle in her I that I remembered from when I was young. It was another cold rainy day and the wind was beating against the house, shaking the squeaky screen door on the front of the house. Arrieal had fallen to sleep in my arms while we were watching the Troll's movie on the new black leather sofa I purchased for my mom.

I was just dozing off when someone began to bang on the front door. My heart began to beat hard in my chest and I didn't want to move from the spot on the sofa. I feared the worst. I knew it was the cops. *I should have never let that woman live.*

Stepping out her bedroom, my mom looked nervous to answer the door as well. "Jermel, I know you hear somebody banging on the door." She waved her hand at me like she didn't want to hear what I had to say and walked to the door in her pink house slippers and matching nightgown. I watched her approach the door and look through the peephole. She jerked back from the door as if she had just been hit then looked at me.

"I know this girl ain't at my door for me." She opened the

door and the pounding of the rain coming down could be heard over the children's movie that played on the TV.

"Get out that rain, child. Come in this house." My mom reached out and pulled the woman into the house.

When I saw her face I was shocked. I don't know how she found me, but she did. It was the girl from the robbery. And her face looked like she had been beaten half to death. She stood in front of the door in her soaked clothes holding her head down, shaking.

"Jermel, come check on her. I'll take Arrieal to my room." After closing the door, my mom crossed the room and picked my daughter up carrying her to her bedroom.

Getting up from the sofa I was kind of confused on why she was here on top of how she was able to find me. She hugged herself tightly as her curly hair was partially hanging over her face but the bruises could still be seen along her jaw and eyes.

"How did you find me? What happened to you? Are you okay?" A storm of questions flew out of my mouth. I didn't know what else to say.

Looking up at me, her face was worse than I thought. Somebody had put a real beating on her. Visions of my mom getting beat when I was young, floated in my head and my anger began to rise. I didn't know why because I didn't even know her, let alone her name. But maybe it was because she saved my life from Tim and felt like I owed her for that.

I grabbed her by her hands circling my thumb in her palms. "You alright, ma?" I sensed something in her I couldn't explain.

Without any warning, she wrapped her arms around me and began to cry. "You said when I sent for you, you would come. I need you now." She was sobbing into my chest.

I pulled her tight to my chest and told her that I had her. It was crazy because I still didn't know her name. But I told her the night of the robbery that I owed her for saving my life and being a man of my word, now that she found me, I felt the obligation to help her. And from the looks of it, she needed me.

"He has been beating me day in and day out. He blamed me for his spot getting robbed." She took a step back and looked me in the eyes. "Jermel, he is going to end up killing me."

I was taken back by the fact she knew my name without me telling her. She obviously had connections throughout the hood being that she found me.

"What do you want me to do, ma? Whatever you need done, I got you." I grabbed ahold of her small hands again.

"I know where he keeps his money at. When I give you the word, I want you to take him for everything and take me away from him." The look on her face told me she was serious. I just knew I had to help her.

"Anything you need me to do, I got you." I didn't even know what I was signing myself up for, but she had saved me from certain death and I had to help her as well.

After letting her borrow a shirt and some shorts, she went into the bathroom and stripped out of her wet clothes. It probably wasn't the time to be lusting but she had a body of a goddess. She caught me looking her up and down and smirked at me. If I was light skinned my cheeks probably would have been rose red. I stepped out of the room and allowed her to get dressed. She came out just as my mom stepped out of her bedroom.

"Melly, could you give me a ride home?" She walked towards the front door. Trying to avoid eye contact with my mom.

"Yeah, I got you. Mom, can you keep an eye on Arrieal while I take..." I looked over to her remembering she never gave me her name.

"Mosuray." She finished my sentence for me.

"Yeah, I will. Take care, sweety. Jermel, you should bring her around more." My mom turned on her heels and walked into the kitchen with a slight grin on her face.

When I looked over to Mosuray, she was smiling. She had a beautiful smile even through all the swelling on her face. I grabbed the keys to Snow's Beamer and threw on my shoes.

Opening the door for her, she talked about how nice my mom seemed. But she stopped in her tracks and leaned back against me when we made it off the steps seeing the all white Range Rover pull into the driveway behind the Beamer.

⚜

The rain had stopped but the clouds still covered the sun making it gloomy out. Snow stepped out of his Range Rover and was on Mosuray in a blink of an eye choking the shit out of her.

"Nigga, you ain't tell me my brother was dead! And now you with this bitch!" His light skin was burning red with anger as he tightened his grip around her neck so hard her eyes looked as if they would pop out her head. He reached his hand high above his head and brought it down, backhanding her. She fell to the wet grass with blood trickling from her nose.

Stepping between the two of them, I grabbed her by the arm lifting her back to her feet. "Nigga, I tried telling you but you were gone off that shit nodding in and out. You weren't hearing shit I said." I hated when niggas put their hands on a woman and how he just did her instantly had my blood boiling.

"Okay, so what you doing with this bitch, nigga? Why isn't she dead?" He barked at me with his fists balled tight.

"She ain't have shit to do with Tim-" Before I could finish what I was saying, he hit her with an open left hand, sending her back to the ground. And was on top of her, choking and smacking her with force. She was screaming in pain trying to kick him off but she struggled against his bigger body.

I tackled Snow off of her and ended up on top of him. I hit him with a left then right hook, causing blood to flow from his mouth. I didn't want to fight my homeboy, but I had no respect for a man who hit a woman. I saw them as pure bitches. I got off of Snow and helped Mosuray to her feet once again.

Tears were raining down her swollen face as the blood from her nose spilled out of her like a faucet. Snow got up, put his hand to his lips then looked at it to see the blood in his hand. He started to reach for his gun but pulled nothing from his hip.

"This what you on, nigga? You gonna choose this bitch over me? You lucky I ain't got my banger on me, nigga." He was backpedaling to his truck now. "I'm gonna be back ho' ass nigga, believe that!" He opened his door and hopped in his whip and smashed off.

"You good, ma?" I asked before wrapping Mosuray into my arms. I felt bad for her. She had been beat before she came to me and now she was just damn near choked to death.

"I'll be okay, but you gotta get me back home before Tony gets back." The blood from her nose had slowed down and I pulled my shirt off and held it to her face.

"Alright, let's go." Walking to the car, I looked back to see my mom in the front window with a concerned look over her face.

I drove Mosuray home and gave her my number before she got out of the car. She told me she would be calling me soon. I let her know I looked forward to hearing from her and headed back to my moms crib.

I still couldn't believe how Snow came at me back at my moms. I would definitely have to holler at the nigga about that. The sun had tried to peek out from the clouds momentarily but it began to sprinkle just as I pulled into the driveway.

❦

Arrieal was sitting on the steps with an angry face on when I got out the car. Walking across the slightly wet grass, I came up to her on the stairs.

"How's my baby doing?" I snatched her up into my arms and spun her around.

Arrieal didn't laugh or even smile so I set her back down on the porch. Something was obviously wrong. "What's wrong,

Arrieal? Talk to Daddy." I kneeled in front of her on the bottom stair as the light rain drizzled on us.

She lowered her head and let out a deep breath. "Granny is smoking again. She always is mean when she smokes." My daughter looked defeated, her shoulders were down and she was looking to the sidewalk as if she was counting how many raindrops hit the ground. My mom didn't smoke cigarettes so I was lost to what was going on.

Stepping past my daughter, I felt my temper rising. The only thing I had ever known my mom to smoke was crack cocaine and as far as I knew she had been clean for over ten plus years. As soon as I opened the door, I knew she was getting high again. The smell of burning crack had a distinct smell. It smelled like burnt sugar in the air.

I must have caught my mom off guard because as soon as she saw me, she dropped the pipe from between her lips. Her eyes were as big as dish plates and sweat was streaming down her face. The glass pipe hit the floor and broke into small pieces and she instantly started to cry with her head down.

I couldn't believe she was smoking crack while my daughter sat outside. I was so taken aback it took a minute for me to snap back into reality.

"So you're smoking that shit again? What the fuck-" She cut me off by standing up and snapping off at me.

"Shut the hell up, Jermel! You don't understand and you never will! You don't know how hard those five years were for me trying to care for your child because you wanted to run the streets. And now you're right back doing the same stuff! So what if I get high from time to time! I'm a grown ass woman!" She snatched up her purse from the table and stormed off to her room.

I went to follow her but her door slammed in my face and I could hear the lock from the other side. I wanted to know how long she had been using. Slowly, it all started to make sense. Now knew why they were living the way they were. My mom had picked up the crack addiction and couldn't stop. The front door closed and I walked back into the living room to find my daughter standing at the entrance of the house.

My baby was only seven and was already having to deal with too much for her age. I hated that my mom was back using crack, but I had my daughter to worry about. I would have to deal with my mom later on. I scooped my daughter into my arms and carried her upstairs to her room.

Setting her on her bed, I sat beside her and held her hand. "Baby, I'm sorry for leaving you before. But I promise you I will never leave you again. Daddy is going to make sure you have everything in the world. I love you, okay?" Tears were beginning to form in my eyes because I didn't know what my daughter had gone through while I was gone and it was my fault for leaving her all those years.

She shook her head, then hugged me tight. I held her close to me and the tears came down my face. We laid in her small bed and she fell to sleep as I looked at the ceiling as if it was going to give me the answers to life. It was up to me to help get my daughter out of this predicament.

As I laid in bed with my daughter, I could hear my mom moving around downstairs. After about an hour, I made my way downstairs to find my mom sitting on the sofa. Her eyes were puffy as if she had been crying and her wig was crooked. I sat next to her and wrapped my arm around her shoulder.

"Momma, I know shit ain't been easy, but I'm home now. You don't have to worry about anything. But I need you to get off that shit. I need you, and your grand baby needs you. I love you, mom." I squeezed her against me tight. She didn't have to say anything to me. I knew that she would get past it. I loved her regardless and I would always be there for her.

CHAPTER 5

IT WAS another three days before Mosuray popped up at my moms crib. The sun was shining bright on this afternoon as birds chirped from above. Mosuray's face was quickly healing and her beauty was again showing.

We were alone at the house because I had sent my daughter and mom to my aunt's crib out in Muskegon after Snow's death threats. I couldn't take him lightly. I knew what he was capable of. Sitting on the leather sofa next to Mosuray, I could tell something was bothering her.

I moved the hair from her face. "What on your mind, Mo?" I turned the volume down on the plasma TV I recently purchased for my moms house.

She put her chin to her chest and looked down at the floor. "I can't keep living like this. I'm sick of living like Tony's dog." A single tear dropped from her eye.

I picked her head up and caressed her cheek looking her in her eye. "You don't have to stay with him. I don't see why you would go back after he beat you. What type of hold does he have on you?" Taking her hand into mine, I pulled her closer to me on the soft leather.

"You wouldn't understand." Looking away from me, her eyes traced over the room.

"Make me understand then. Tell me why you are so stuck on him." I genuinely wanted to know why she hadn't left him. He obviously was holding something against her.

Her hazel eyes met mine and her face expression saddened. "Tony has been around since I was a little girl. No more than twelve years old." I could see the tears forming in her eyes. "My mom has been addicted to heroin since before I could remember and that's where he comes in." Her light skin was now flushed red. "My mom ran up a debt so deep she sold me to Tony when I was fourteen years old. And since then, I've basically been a slave to him." She broke down in tears and laid her head against my chest.

I allowed her to get all the tears out herself as I held her tight. In my head, I imagined my daughter without me there for her and what would become of her with my moms addiction.

"Tony is gross. He first started forcing me to have sex with him shortly after my fifteenth birthday." Her tears had stopped falling and I could hear the anger build up in her voice. "At first, I wouldn't allow the nigga to touch me and that's when he began to beat me like I was a grown ass man. If he was mad, he would take it out on me. My mom was so far gone into her heroin addiction and so scared of him, she never said or did anything about it." She took a deep breath and exhaled. "He has pimped me out to his friends before. Tony doesn't give a fuck about anything, but himself. I've tried to commit suicide a number of times. I always stop short thinking that I would leave my mom to be stuck with him."

I kissed her forehead and allowed her to get all her feelings out. I was getting hot thinking about what she had to go through as a young girl. I wanted to kill that Tony nigga for what he had done to her. My mind was already processing ways I could do it.

Wrapping her arms around my waist she stopped crying. "For most of my life I've been raped and beaten daily by Tony. He has done things to me that I will never be able to get over. And the same things he does to me, he does to my mom, too. I want to run away from it but then he has my mom still." She wiped the tears from her face.

"But she is the one who sold you to him, why would you care if she was stuck with him?" I didn't understand why she would care about the lady who put her in the horrible situation in the first place.

She sat up and looked me into my eyes. "You only have one mom and I don't blame her for the way things are. Tony was also the one who got her hooked on heroin. He forced it into her arm along with a couple of her friends. That's how Tony got his clientele when he first started selling."

I was damn near in tears as she told me her story on why she hadn't left Tony yet. I felt so bad for her and even her mom. I didn't think that any woman or child should have been treated any less then like a precious diamond. Tony was a monster. I wondered if he would come to a grown nigga like that or if he was a bitch made ass nigga who only preyed on females.

She looked down to the floor again and took a deep breathe. "He told me that he will do me the same way once he is done having his way with me. I can't take it anymore. I have to get my mom outta there and get away from Grand Rapids. I have almost ten thousand dollars saved up and I know where he keeps his money, too. If we can-"

Her phone vibrated in her jeans causing her to stop talking. "It's my mom, hold on." Sliding her thumb across the screen she answered the phone.

She bucked her eyes and I could see she was either angry or worried. "Mom, what's wrong? Where are you?" She stood up and was damn near screaming into the phone. "Mom! Mom! Hello?" She looked at the phone as if it had hit her in her face.

"My mom... needs me.. She said she was.... Can you please take me to get my mom?" She could barely form a whole sentence and I could see fear creep over her body.

Standing up with her, I began to worry for her mother even though I didn't know her. "What's going on?" She was already walking towards the front door.

Without turning around, she opened the door while saying that she just needed to get to her mom fast. I followed her out the house and jumped into my moms Volkswagen Jetta. I had dropped Snow's car off around the corner after his threat. I wasn't going to openly go to his house. He still hadn't tried anything, but I took all threats seriously coming from the hood.

Mosuray couldn't stop shaking her legs as I sped through the hood to the house I had dropped her off to previously. The night was cold and the streets were damn near empty. Mosuray was so shaky I was beginning to get nervous as well.

"Chill ma, it's going to be alright." I didn't know if that was true or not but I was trying to calm her down. For her sake, I silently prayed that her mom was okay. After what she had told me, I didn't know how much more she could take.

❦

As soon as I hit the block Tony's house was on, we saw three niggas with machine guns come running out the crib. They all had masks on and one was carrying a duffle bag. I had known Snow for a long time and even while wearing a mask I could point him out. I knew his movements and when they jumped into a white Range Rover and smashed off I knew it was him for sure.

"Oh shit! Somebody just robbed the house!" Mosuray clicked off her seatbelt and was already reaching for the door handle.

The fear that something bad had just happened to Mosuray's mom hit a new height. Snow was just like me when it came to licks, anything breathing inside was supposed to be breathless when we left the crib. So if her mom was in the house chances were she was no longer living.

Pulling to the curb in front of the house, Mosuray jumped

out the car before it completely stopped. She nearly tripped when her feet hit the dead grass in front of the house. I got out of the car following her as she climbed the crooked steps and came to the wide open door to the old style blue house. The door was halfway off its hinges from being kicked in.

Stepping into the living room, the smell of gunpowder was heavy in the air. The couch was flipped onto the cushion part and the seats were ripped open. There was cotton from the inside all over the living room and the TV had been broken. I knew things weren't going to be good. Mosuray ran to a room on the left side of the hallway that ran the length of the house. She was only in the room shortly before she flew across the small hallway into another room. She came out and stopped in front of me, breathing like she had just run a hundred meter dash.

"Maybe she got away. She is normally in her room, right there." She pointed to the open door she had just come out of. She stepped back into the first room she went into and looked back to me. "I hope whoever kicked the door in didn't find my stash."

I walked down the hall into the kitchen to find that it had also been trashed. The food from the cabinets were scattered all over the floor. Silverware was also thrown onto the floor. Snow came looking for something. I only hoped Mosuray's mom had made it out of the house before he found her as well.

Mosuray came running up the hallway carrying a small bag in her hands. "They didn't find my money I was saving." She glanced around the kitchen with a disgusted look on her face. "I'm gonna try to call my mom. I think she must have gotten away." I could see that she was still worried about her mom.

She pulled out her phone and dialed her mom's number. The house was completely silent and I could hear the ringing coming through her phone as she waited for her mom to answer. The ringing stopped and I could hear the answering machine tell her to leave a message.

"She's not answering. My mom always answers my calls." She

dialed back the number. I could see that she was on the verge of crying. We walked up the hallway towards the living room passing a set of stairs that went up.

"What's up there?" I looked up the stairs next to the room I figured was hers.

She was focused on her phone, sending her mom a text message. "Tony's room is up there. I only been up there a couple times in all the years we have been here." She was typing rapidly on her phone.

I climbed halfway up the creaking wooden stairs before the smell of blood seeped into my nostrils. It smelled like a bunch of copper pennies. I knew it had to be a lot of blood from how strong the smell was. When I got to the top of the stairs I damn near had to plug my nose from the stench. I saw two big bullet holes in the wall by the closed door.

There were only two doors upstairs and one was already open and I could see it was a small bathroom. I stepped to the second door and already knew that what was on the other side couldn't be good. Blood was coming from under the door. I slowly twisted the knob on the door and pushed it open. It opened about eight inches and stopped. I took a step back and was frozen in that spot. The door wouldn't open anymore because of the dead body behind it.

"Melly! Melly, what are you doing up there?" I could hear Mosuray calling out to me but I was so lost from what I was looking at, my brain couldn't put together any words to respond to her.

I heard her step onto the bottom of the stairs. "You hear me? She still isn't answering my calls. I don't know where she would be and Tony isn't answering either." She started to come up the stairs.

I stood looking into the room hearing Mosuray come up the stairs. I didn't know why I was so taken back by what I was looking at. I had killed multiple niggas in my days in the streets. But for some reason I felt anger inside my heart. Like I was cheated out of something. Mosuray made it to the top of the stairs and looked at me with a confused look on her face.

"I know you fucking heard me. We gotta find my mom, Melly."

I simply looked over at her then back into the room without responding.

"Why you just standing there looking into his room Mel-" Her words came up short as she stepped to my side.

It was like things didn't come together for her for almost a full minute as she stared blankly into the room just as I had been doing before she dropped down to her knees into the blood that had come under the door. Tears came flooding down her face. All I could do was kneel behind her and rub her back. I didn't know what she was feeling.

Tony's body was twisted right by the door so that it barely could open. His face was looking towards us with big open eyes. There was a big hole in the middle of his forehead and blood was still slowly coming out of it. His mouth was wide open and the back of his head looked like it had been blown off.

"He's dead, Mosuray. You're free from him now. It's okay." I wrapped my arms around her shoulder as she continued to cry.

"I never thought this would happen. I'm so happy that he is dead." She put her hand on top of mine and slowly stood up. "Now we gotta find my mom."

She pushed the door against his body, opening it enough to step into. Before I could catch her, she fell to the floor screaming. "NOOOOOO!" She sobbed uncontrollably as she sat slumped on her butt looking across the room.

I stepped over Tony's head and looked in the direction Mosuray was looking in and instantly became nauseous.

"No! No! No!" She hollered out.

All I could do was sit at her side. She was going to need someone to lean on.

CHAPTER 6

Mosuray continued to break down as I held on to her. Sitting against the wall in the room was the mutilated body of an older light skinned woman who I assumed was her mom. Blood was splattered all over the room and it looked as if she had been tortured.

Her right hand was missing two fingers and her left hand was completely gone. Snow had always been one to kill someone slowly so they could basically see themselves die. But the most horrific part of it was the top of her skull was completely gone. It looked like a bowl of tomato soup was sitting on top of her head spilling over her face.

Looking away from her body, I saw five yellow shotgun shells beside the flipped over bed. Tony must have finally told Snow and his goons where the money was and that's when he most likely killed them both.

There were clothes everywhere and the dresser was tipped on its side. Blood covered the majority of the room. The sight of the small room would be something I would never be able to get out of my head. I was on the verge of throwing up from the smell of blood in the air.

I couldn't imagine what was going on in Mosuray's mind. No more than thirty minutes ago, she was speaking to her mom on the phone and now she was looking at her dead body.

Hooking my arm into hers, I helped her to her feet. "I'm sorry, Mo, but we gotta go." I turned her towards the door and stepped over Tony's body, helping her down the stairs.

Once we made it to my moms car, I helped her inside then got behind the wheel. She was looking at the house with tears flowing down her pretty face as I pulled away from the curb, speeding through the quiet night back towards my moms house. The radio was off and through the cracked window the wind whistled into the car blowing her curly hair around.

It was a silent ride back to my moms crib besides the sound of Mosuray crying. I couldn't find any words that would help her in a time like this. And if it was me in her shoes, I don't know how I would have reacted.

I was going to make sure I stuck by her side though. No matter what, I would be there for her. After she told me all she had gone through since she was a young teen, I couldn't imagine her life getting any worse and now this had happened. I felt like she needed me even more. The moon was sitting high in the sky and stars speckled the night giving a light glow to the darkness. It had been a sad night and with Snow still breathing, I didn't know when things would be back to normal. I knew I had to be strong for Mosuray after what she had just seen.

❧

When we made it back to my house, I basically carried Mosuray inside. The tears had stopped but her body seemed to have shut down. I carried her to my room and set her on the bed and pulled her shoes off her feet. Her pants were covered in blood, so I helped her out of them and gave her a pair of my sweat-pants. She still hadn't said a word since we found her mother dead.

After putting on the sweats, she laid in the bed looking up at the ceiling. I turned to leave out the room to give her space.

"Can you hold me please, Melly?" She turned her head to look at me as I was opening the door.

Letting go of the door, I stepped back over to the bed. "Anything you need me to do, I got you." Slipping out of my shoes I climbed into the small bed with her.

As I settled into the bed with her I wrapped my arms around her with her back to my chest as her body molded into mine. I kissed her neck as I held tightly to her body.

"I got you, ma. I'm here for you." I whispered into her ear.

She turned over in my arms so that she was facing me and looked me in the eyes. Her hazel eyes appeared to be looking for something as she scanned my face. Her soft lips met mine and I pulled her closer to me as our tongues danced with each other.

Her hand rubbed on my chest under my shirt as I explored her body with my own hands. Rubbing down her back all the way to gripping her juicy ass. I could feel my manhood rising as we continued to tongue box.

Pulling her lips away from mine, she was breathing heavily. "Make me forget about the pain, Melly. I need you to take me away." She pulled her shirt off exposing her round titties that sat up in her Victoria's Secret bra.

I stood out of the bed and quickly undressed myself with the help of her. When my shirt came off, she trailed my abs with her soft hands down to my waistline. She pulled my sweats and boxers down together leaving my dick sticking straight up in the air. I removed the pants and boxers from around my legs and tossed them to the side.

Mosuray had already pulled the sweats off and was now laying on the bed rubbing the center of her panties that barely covered her fat sex lips. I could see the soft fabric between her legs getting moist as she continued to apply pressure to her box.

I dropped to my knees at the edge of the bed and pulled her to me by her ankles. Planting my face into her box, I tried to suck the juices out of her through her panties causing her to lightly moan before I ripped them off her.

Spreading her legs wide, I began to twist my tongue around her clit. I could feel her juices dripping down my chin as I continued to work on her button.

"Mmmm! Shit yes!" She bucked her hips into me as my tongue slipped into her wet center and my finger flicked her clit.

The smell of her was driving me crazy as I licked her pussy like a thirsty dog. Her legs began to shake. I knew she was on the verge of coming. Sliding two fingers into her tight pussy, I put her clit between my lips and pulled it. My fingers were slowly going in and out of her while I played with her clit with my tongue.

"I'm.. Oooohh shit, I'm commmminnnnggggg!" She screamed out as her juices began to squirt out her box onto the bottom of my face.

I pulled my fingers out of her pussy and put my face in her slit and began to slurp up all of her juices as it poured out of her. She grabbed the back of my head pushing my face into her cat as I continued to lick her pussy until I brought her to another climax.

"Now take the pain away." She said as she circled around her erect nipples with her finger tips.

Standing at the edge of the bed, I grabbed the back of her thighs and pushed her knees to her chest. Her pussy poked up at me as her juices trailed down into her ass crack. I guided my dick into her box slowly as a light moan came from her sexy lips. Sinking myself slowly into her tight pussy, my balls slapped her ass before I began to stroke her with every inch of me.

Her mouth was wide open and she was squeezing her eyes closed as I fucked her slowly making sure she felt every bit of me inside of her. I began to speed up my strokes plunging deep into her womb. My balls slapped against her ass like hands clapping as I increased the speed of my strokes.

"Oooohh, yesssss! Fuck me harder, Melly! Mmmmm!" Her pussy muscles tightened around the base of my dick as I gave her all I had.

I wanted to help her escape from the pain she was feeling. Pulling out of her wetness, I roughly flipped her onto her stomach and spread her ass cheeks apart exposing the pink of her pussy. Then buried my face in her pussy from the back. She gripped the sheets on the bed and arched her back into the air.

"Yesss! Make me come again! Eat my pussy, baby!" She was spread eagle on her stomach.

I ate her pussy like that until she began to come again before I grabbed her by her hips pulling her to her knees. Her fat ass was tooted in the air as she bust it wide open for me. Positioning myself behind her, I stroked my dick as I smacked her on the ass twice. I could see her juices dripping off her fat pussy lips.

I rammed my dick into her hard causing her to scream and started to beat her walls in with force.

"Take the pain away! Yesss! Mmmmm!" She moaned looking back at me.

I gripped her hips as she threw her ass back to take every inch I had for her. She moaned out in pleasure. All the sexy noises she made only encouraged me to fuck her harder. Pushing my hand down on her lower back, I started to hit her spot and could feel her warm juices squirting out her pussy.

Feeling my balls tighten underneath me, I started to pound into her core like a jackhammer until I exploded deep inside her walls. I pulled out of her wet pussy and she quickly turned over and took me into her mouth bringing my dick back to its full mass.

"Oohh shit!" She sucked me to the base of my dick while she cupped my balls.

Taking me out her mouth, she looked up at me and spit on my dick and licked the head before sucking me back into her throat. She continued to go up and down on me until my toes curled and I shot my warm load down her throat. She milked me for everything I had before she took her lips off me, stood off the bed and kissed my lips.

"Thank you. Now, can you just hold me?" She pulled me onto the bed.

Wrapping my arms around her, I kissed her forehead and pulled her to my chest. We both laid in the bed tired from the whole day and sex we just had. As she laid against my body, she fell to sleep with our bodies tangled together. I held her in my arms listening to her light snore as I thought about all she had been through. I felt the need to protect her. I told myself I would do everything to make sure she was straight from this day out. The warmth of her body against mine was comforting and felt natural. Her scent lingered in the air consuming me.

I could hear the wind whistling outside my bedroom window as I laid in the bed looking up at the ceiling. I damn near felt responsible for the death of her mother. If I hadn't talked Snow into putting me on a lick then things would have never escalated to this. But I also wouldn't have had Mosuray in my arms. So I was feeling bad about her mom dying, but I was happy to be holding onto her.

I don't know how I would have reacted to finding my mom with the top of her head missing. The streets wouldn't be safe until I found the person responsible. Snow was to blame for the pain she had just gone through. I didn't know if she wanted to get revenge for her mom, but I was down to help her if that's what she wanted to do.

Snow had threatened my life and I already felt some type of way about that. So if she wanted to get back at him that would only add fuel to the fire that was burning inside me. I had to get Snow before he came through on the promise to kill me. I knew how the streets were and it was a dog eat dog world. If you weren't willing to kill, then the streets weren't for you. But I was raised in the streets. I was the definition of a savage. Since my early teens, I had been causing hell all through my city. I know Snow was somewhat about that life, but I was on a whole different level.

CHAPTER 7

MOSURAY WOKE up screaming and kicking me off her in the middle of the night. Jumping out the bed, I turned on the bedside lamp. She was sitting on the bed with her knees to her chest shaking with tears streaming down her cheeks. She looked like she had seen a ghost.

I sat next to her on the edge of the bed wrapping my arm around her. "You having nightmares, baby?" I kissed the side of her head.

"It was a dream about my mom. I just saw the killing happen in my dream and after he killed my mom he turned the gun to me. And I started to scream. That's when I woke up." Her body was tense and she was crying into her folded arms.

"I'm sorry, Mo. I know this shit can't be easy to deal with, but I'm here with you, ma." I hugged her into my chest.

"I don't want to go back to sleep, Melly. Can you stay up with me please?" She looked at me with her sad hazel eyes. There was no way I could tell her no at a time like this. She needed someone to be there for her, and right now that someone was me.

I stood up from the bed and went to my dresser to grab some boxers and some shorts and a tee shirt for her. Handing her the shorts and shirt after I put my boxers on, I lifted her from the bed.

"I got you, ma. Let's go into the living room and chill then."

While she got dressed, I went into the kitchen and grabbed two bowls from the cabinet and the family size box of Captain Crunch cereal. After making us both a fat ass bowl of Crunch Berries, I carried it to the living room where she was sitting on the couch.

"When I was little, my mom always made me my favorite cereal when I had nightmares." I set the bowls on the coffee table in front of her. We ate cereal like two kids before school in the morning. After I finished, I slurped up the milk out the bowl. Mosuray began to laugh at me. It was nice to see her smile for a change.

It was almost four in the morning when I looked at the old cuckoo clock on the wall my mom had since I was a little boy. As we sat on the couch after eating our cereal, she laid down with her head on my lap. I took her hand into mine and I could feel a connection between us that I had never felt before.

"So, tell me what little Melly wanted to be as a young boy?" She looked up at me with her puffy hazel eyes smiling.

Smiling back at her, I thought about my childhood briefly. "Man, as a child, I was just Jermel. But I was the young kid in the hood who always had a basketball with him. I swore I was the next Kobe Bryant or LeBron James. All I wanted to do was play ball all day long."

"So, why you stop?" She asked as her thumb rubbed the palm of my hand.

"You getting serious, huh?" I laughed. "Well, when I turned fourteen I sold weed for the first time and from there, I graduated to getting fast money and gave up on my hoop dreams." Looking at the TV for a moment, I thought about what I could have been.

"Shortly after, I started selling dope. I did my first robbery and it came so natural to me that I turned into a stick up kid. I was a savage with my shit too. if I had to body you, I did that. By any means, I was going to get what I came for. I ended up doing eighteen months in juvie and when I got out from there I went straight back to robbing niggas up until I went to prison."

Looking down at her, I moved the hair from her face. "Now, what about you? What did you want to be as a youngin'?"

The slight smile disappeared from her face. "Umm, I don't know. As a young girl, I wanted to be a princess like every other little girl." She took a deep breath and exhaled. "But I was sold to Tony before I had any idea what I wanted to be in life. And if I did have any dreams, he broke those right away with the things he did to me. As I approached my young teen years, the only thing I only wanted to do was survive." Tears were starting to build in her eyes again.

I kissed her forehead and changed the subject. "So, what is your favorite color?" I smiled at her trying to lighten the mood.

"Blue of course, the color of the sky on a beautiful day." She gave me a smirk. "You?"

"I like the color orange. I don't know why maybe because it looks good on my chocolate skin." I teased.

She slapped my chest and laughed. "Oh, you think you're fine?" She smiled.

Leaning my head to the side, I shrugged my shoulders. "I mean, I'm a light ten."

She busted out laughing in my lap. "You think you the shit." She sat up on the couch and kissed me. "You alright I guess."

"You ain't that bad yourself, ma." I nudged her with my shoulder. "So tell me, if you could live anywhere in the world where would it be?"

"That's a good one. Hmm, damn I don't even know. I never thought about it. How about you?" She leaned up against me.

"I don't know. California or Florida. Somewhere that doesn't have winter cause I hate the snow." The TV was showing a video of a dog riding on a skateboard. I laughed at the thought of seeing something like that in the hood.

"I always wanted a dog. But yeah your right, I don't like the cold either. But the Fall and Spring in Michigan is so beautiful to me. I love when the trees turn that bright orange. It's so warm." She closed her eyes as if she was imagining the autumn orange of the Oak trees.

I got up from the couch and walked over to the radio and put in one of my moms CD's. The smooth sound of Musiq Soul Child came out the surround sound speakers, filling the room. Walking back over to the couch, I reached my hand out for her. "Dance with me, Mo." Pulling her from the couch into my arms, I kissed her soft lips.

"I don't know how to really slow dance." She said as I hugged her against my body.

"Shit, I don't either but we can learn together." We stepped over to the open space by the front door. I held onto her waist with one hand and with her soft hand in my other, we began to sway back and forth to the music. Looking into her eyes, I was losing myself in her.

Following my steps, she hugged me tight, laying her head on my shoulder. "So, what happened to your baby momma?"

My hand slid from her waist down to her ass. "Arrieal's mom left her with me when she was only a few months old. She didn't want to have the responsibility of a child. We were young and she didn't want to give up her freedom I guess. And since then, it's been me, my daughter and my mom." I rarely talked about my baby momma but with Mosuray I felt comfortable and wanted to share myself with her.

"Arrieal. I like that name, who named her?" She asked as we spun in a circle to the soothing sound of the music.

"My baby momma did. I guess she liked the Little Mermaid." I laughed.

Leaning her head, she looked at my scrunching her eyebrows. "Don't laugh, I loved the Little Mermaid and I love your baby's name."

I put my hands in the air, surrendering. "I love her name, too.

I'm just not a big fan of the Little Mermaid. I'm a Space Jam type guy." We continued to try and dance to the music.

I almost tripped over her feet once or twice before I called it quits with the slow dance. Mosuray was smiling though and that's what mattered to me the most. I just wanted to take her mind off what had happened the night before.

We both sunk into the couch laughing together. Neither one of us could dance, but I enjoyed it and she seemed to as well. "I ain't slow danced with a woman since my grandma used to stand me on her feet, and two-step around the house to the old music she used to listen to." A smile crossed my face as I was thinking about my grandma.

"Awe, that's sweet. Is she still alive?" She asked, leaning up against me as I threw my arm around her shoulder.

"Naw, my grandma passed away about seven years ago from bone cancer. But she lived a happy life and made everyone she came across smile as well." Leaning my head to hers, I could smell a light scent of apple shampoo.

"Yeah, that's how my grandma was, too. But she died when I was only eleven. That's when my mom started to use drugs. And from there, it went down hill. My grandma was the glue that held my mom together I guess you could say. And losing her, that's what threw her over the deep end." Her voice got a little shaky when she talked about her mom. "I know she wasn't the best mom, but she was mine. I'm going to miss her."

I pulled her in tight. "I'm sorry, ma. You shouldn't have to go through this. But know I'm here with you."

She looked at me and pressed her lips to mine sucking my bottom lips into her mouth and lightly biting it. "Thank you, Jermel."

"You ain't gotta thank me ma, I got you. I told you before, you saved my life and I'll forever be in debt to you for what you did that night." Pressing my lips against hers, I kissed her again.

It was hard to believe that just over a month ago I had saved her from being raped and she saved me from being murdered. I guess through what happened that night in Tony's trap, we formed a bond that brought us together. I was happy with the way things worked out because I was beginning to feel some type of way towards Mosuray.

"I'm going to get something to drink. You want some kool-aid?" I asked getting up from the couch walking towards the kitchen.

"Don't bring me no white people kool-aid, Melly." She laughed.

She just didn't know how sweet my mom's kool-aid. It was enough to give a person diabetes. I poured us both a big glass of Grape kool-aid putting four ice cubes into hers and brought it back to the living room.

"These videos are goofy as hell. And thank you." She was watching the TV that was showing funny videos.

I watched her take a sip of the kool-aid. "Now, that's some kool-aid!" She smacked her lips with a smile.

"Yeah, moms make the best kool-aid. I think she put a whole bag of sugar in a pitcher." I laughed before taking a few gulps out my glass as I sat beside her.

"Melly, I want him dead." She said simply, breaking the brief silence.

"You talking about Snow?"

She nodded.

"I got you, baby. I'll handle that for you." I was waiting for her to say that's what she wanted.

She looked me in my eyes and I could tell she was serious. And I was serious about killing Snow for her.

She shook her head from side to side. "No, I want to do it myself. He took my mom from me, Melly. I want to be the one who takes his life away. I always prayed that my mom would come from under her addiction and we would escape Tony. And he took those dreams from me. He took away the hope I had for a better life for me and my mom. And I want him to pay for that." Tears were building up in her eyes and I could see the pain come back to her.

"Okay, if that's what you want then that's what's going to happen." A single tear fell from her eye and I wiped it away with my thumb.

I did not know how we would get at Snow, but there would have to be a way. I wanted him dead just as bad as she did.

"I won't be able to sleep until I know he isn't running around the streets. I...I just gotta make things even." She laid her head back against my lap.

She had killed Tim, but her reaction after shooting him told me that was her first time killing someone. I'm sure she had a hard time sleeping many nights after that. I didn't know if she was ready to take another life but I would be there to make sure he was dead if she couldn't pull the trigger herself. No matter what, I was going to be sure Snow was dead because I also wouldn't sleep well knowing he was breathing after he had threatened my life.

"I understand, baby. We're gonna take care of him when the time is right. We can't go about it without a plan. We will get him though believe me." I was rubbing her back looking at the TV that was on mute it was playing funny videos of animals. The sound of Musiq Soul Child still filled the house.

"I never had someone who I felt cared for me before. But for some reason I feel safe with you Melly."

"That's good cause I'm going to make sure you are good from here on out. I never cared about anyone other than my daughter, my mom and myself. But I find myself caring for you already." I wasn't the type to get emotional but Mosuray was doing something to me.

It was damn near five-thirty in the morning and the sun started to rise and was beginning to turn the sky purplish pink. We fell to sleep on the couch, me sitting up and her laying across my lap as the music sung us to sleep. I dreamed about seeing her pull the trigger that would send the bullet into Snow's skull that would kill him. I could see the smile on her face knowing she had avenged her mother's death.

After sitting up with her for those hours, I had some of the best sleep I had ever had. I don't know what had come over me, but I was willing to risk my life for Mosuray. She now held a special place in my heart, and I would never allow her to want or need for anything as long as I held oxygen in my lungs.

CHAPTER 8

AFTER THE NIGHT we found Mosuray's mom, Mosuray and I had been glued to each other. For seven days straight, we had been inseparable, and I felt genuinely happy for the first time in my life. It was something about Mosuray that made me feel special.

We had been chilling in the crib since it was raining, watching a Tyler Perry movie and eating Hot Cheetos and Mike and Ikes in the living room.

"Baby, this man, Tyler Perry, is crazy." She laughed. "I don't know how he came up with these Madea movies but he's funny as hell." She popped a few Cheetos into her mouth.

I grabbed the couple chips from her hand and tossed them in my mouth. "For real, cause Madea is crazy." I busted out laughing as the old lady on the TV was whooping a young kid with her purse.

Mosuray laid across my lap and put her fingers in her mouth sucking off the red Cheeto stains from her fingertips. "That reminds me of-" Her words were cut off from her phone ringing loud on the coffee table.

She picked her phone up and a picture of a dark skin chick appeared on the screen. "Oh, it's my friend Shanae." She slid her thumb across the screen to answer the call then put it on speaker phone.

"Shanae, what's up girl?" She sat up on the couch as I paused the movie.

"Girl, you remember you told me a nigga named Snow killed your mom?" Mosuray's eyes damn near popped out of her head. Even I leaned forward to hear what her friend was going to say.

"Yeah, I remember. Why, what's up?" She was holding the phone close to her face.

"Okay, so look, the nigga seen me at the club tonight and invited me back to his hotel room. I left with him and he got high and started talking about how he killed some nigga named-"

Mosuray cut her off. "Shanae, what's up? I know you ain't call me to tell me you fucked the nigga that killed my mom!" Mosuray's temper was rising. I put my hand on her back to calm her down.

"Girl, hell naw! This nigga is so high on something he was snorting. He is half dead on the bed. Girl, you can come do whatever you need to do. I hit his pockets already and I'm about to leave. He ain't got a gun or nothing, so I'm just trying to help you out. I know Melly about that life." Obviously Mosuray had told her friend that we had been fucking around.

"Where y'all at?" Mosuray was already standing up as if she was ready to shoot out the front door.

"We at the DoubleTree on 28th street. Room 303. I'm going to leave the key card by the door." Shanae was a true friend. I knew her from around the city before I wet to prison as a chick who set niggas up to get robbed. So I wasn't surprised that she ended up with Snow at a hotel.

"Alright girl, I owe you."

"Be safe girl. Call me later or something." Mosuray hung up the phone with a devilish look in her eyes.

Mosuray looked at me and I could see the hate for Snow she

was feeling boiling inside her. I already knew what she was going to say before she said it. "I'm ready Melly. I want him dead."

I stood up and looked her in her face. "I told you baby, I will be with you until the end. If this is what you want to do, I'll be by your side." Wrapping my arms around her, I hugged her tight.

She had made her mind up. I knew she wasn't a cold blooded killer like I was. But in the name of her mother, I knew she would be able to handle her business and body Snow. Shanae had said he was half dead off something he was snorting. So I knew he was high on heroin just like the night me and his brother Tim hit the lick on Tony's spot. And if he was anywhere close to as high as he was that night, this would be easier then Sunday morning like the old song said.

"Let's go then, baby, so you can put this all behind you." Letting her go we walked to my room. Mosuray's entire mood had changed after receiving the call from her friend. I don't know what was going through her mind. I knew it was a lot to take in. We both dressed in all black and I put on a black baseball hat over my waves to hide my face. I grabbed the .45 I had got from Snow on the first night I got out of prison and tucked it into my waistband.

After we got dressed, we walked through the house and out the front door. Mosuray still hadn't said anything and was holding a serious look on her face. Walking across the yard to the car, I grabbed Mosuray's arm, turning her towards me as we stood in the rain.

"Mo, you don't have to do this. I will handle it for you." I was holding her with both hands by her elbows.

"No...No..I have to do this, Jermel. I want him to look me in the face and know it was me who killed him." She pulled away from me, walked around the car and got in without saying another word. I was riding with her regardless. I got into the driver's seat and pulled off into the rain.

Pulling up to the DoubleTree the rain was coming down so hard, I could barely see out the window. I parked the car on the side of the building and cut the lights off leaving the car running. Pulling out the gun, I cocked back the slide to put a bullet into the chamber and handed it to Mosuray.

"Let's go, baby." I opened the door just as a loud crash of thunder erupted and lighting struck, illuminating the night sky for a millisecond. We ran to the side door of the building and quickly made our way to the stairs. We raced up the stairs to the third floor as fast as we could. The room Snow was in was at the end of the hallway, so once we made it to the third floor we had to run down the hall to his door.

Stopping at room 303, I lifted up the flower pot next to the door and found the room key card Mosuray's friend had left for us.

"You ready, baby?" I asked looking back at Mosuray as I prepared to slide the card into the door to unlock it.

Mosuray looked down at the gun hanging in her right hand then nodded to me. I slid the key into the door and snatched it open. Mosuray rushed into the room holding the gun up ready to shoot. I followed her into the room where we found Snow laid out on the bed snoring with drool coming out his mouth onto the plush pillows on the bed.

On the small dresser beside the bed, was a plate with a couple lines of tan heroin laid out on it along with the room phone. I stepped to the bed and Snow didn't move. Disconnecting the phone from the wall, I took the phone cord that plugged into the wall and pointed to the wooden chair by the window.

Mosuray slid the chair over to me. I tossed her the cord then grabbed Snow who was so high on heroin he didn't wake up at all as I moved him into the chair where I tied his ankles up to the chair with the cord. Using a sheet, I wrapped it around his body tying it behind his back so he couldn't move his arms. It wasn't the best restraints but it would have to work.

Mosuray grabbed the remote from the bed and powered on the TV turning the volume up to the max. Once she stood back in front of Snow, I reached back and smacked him across his face.

Snow's eyes popped open to see Mosuray pointing the barrel of the gun directly at his nose. He was so high his eyes slowly closed as if he didn't see what was happening. I reached back and smacked him again, this time when his eyes opened they stayed open.

"What the fuck is going on?" He was looking at Mosuray but even from the side I could see the fear in his eyes.

Mosuray flipped out and started yelling. "You killed my mom! The only person in this world I had and you took her away from me!" Her hands were shaking as she held the gun on him. "I'll never be able to tell her how much I loved her because of you. I'll never get to see her happy and it's your fault." Mosuray was breathing like she just ran a marathon.

"You ain't no killer, you just a little ho'." Snow looked over to me as I stood beside him. "And yo' bitch ass gonna help this bitch kill me!" He tried to spit on me but missed.

"Your brother didn't think I would have killed him either. But where is he now?" Mosuray had tears falling down her face as the anger in her voice continued to rise.

"Fuck you, bitch! Get it over with and pull the trigger then!" He was screaming at the top of his lungs, but the sound of the TV was muffling the sound of his voice. I punched him in his jaw causing a little blood to come from his bottom lip. I stepped behind Mosuray as she aimed the gun at Snow.

"Fuck you! Fuck you!" Mosuray yelled.

I thought she was going to pull the trigger, but her hands were shaking so bad it looked like she was going to drop the gun.

I know her emotions had to be everywhere facing off with Snow. She told me she wanted to be the one to kill him, so I was going to help her through it.

Positioning myself behind her, I wrapped my arms around her and helped her steady the gun. "Breathe baby, just breathe." Her hands stopped shaking and she took a deep breath. Snow continued to yell at the top of his lungs. I moved her finger to the trigger then let her go and took a step back.

BOOM!

She squeezed the trigger, sending a bullet crashing into Snow's forehead. His head snapped back hard before falling forward and laid on his chest with blood leaking from his forehead.

Mosuray dropped the gun and began to cry as she looked at the body of her mother's killer. Stepping back to her, I wrapped my arms around her and hugged her tightly as she continued to cry. Mosuray had to feel a sense of relief, and I know she felt at least a little happy to know that her mom's killer was now dead. I kissed her forehead as she leaned back and looked me in my eyes.

"Las Vegas. I would live in Las Vegas if I could move anywhere." She said leaning back into me.

After picking up the gun from the floor, we ran out the hotel room down the hall and down the stairs. Rushing out the hotel, we got to the car and smashed off. Snow was now dead and we could move on with our lives without the worry of him hunting us down. Mosuray had gotten her revenge in the name of mother and hopefully, she could put the past behind her. Driving back to my moms, the rain stopped as if signaling that the bad times were over. Mosuray took my hand in her as she leaned her head back on the seat.

"I love you, Jermel." She looked at me as I drove down 28th street towards the hood.

"I love you, too, baby." It was the first time I told a woman besides my mom or my daughter, that I loved them. But I truly meant it when I told her that I loved her. After hearing her story and spending time with her, I knew I couldn't be without her in my life.

When we made it to my moms, Mosuray went straight to my bedroom where she instantly fell asleep. This time, she slept through the whole night peacefully. I slept next to her holding her in my arms. The next chapter in our lives was just starting and it looked promising.

One year later...

As I drove, Mosuray slept in the backseat next to the car seat of our son. Mosuray had got pregnant the first time we had sex and here we were twelve months later with a three month old son, Jermel Jr. Mosuray and Arrieal became best friends. Arrieal loved her and she loved Arrieal.

I always felt like there was something special about Mosuray and with each day that passed by, my love for her grew. Mosuray told me after she killed Snow that she would move to Las Vegas if she could live anywhere.

So here we were, driving on the highway to Nevada. Who knows what life will have in store for us out there, but with Mosuray by my side, I knew things would be good. She was the love of my life and even though we met under difficult circumstances, at the end of the day we love each other and that's all that mattered.

Arrieal was so happy to have a woman she could look up to. And I was looking forward to the new start in Las Vegas. I left the street life back in Grand Rapids and hoped to make something out of myself in Las Vegas. As I looked in the rearview mirror at Mosuray, Arrieal and our son, I saw new found happiness in my life. It came with a price, but I now had a queen by my side to give all the love a thug had to give.

The end

NOTE FROM AUTHOR

On behalf of J-TWO, T & J Publications would like to thank you all for giving this gentleman a try. Though incarcerated, we wanted to offer him a chance to showcase his writing talents and hope you continue to support him.

Thanks again for taking the time to show support.
Stay updated on TJP's latest releases by joining our reading group.
www.facebook.com/groups/tjpreaderz/